CEDS
P9-BYF-101

Baby High, Baby Low

for Jordie - S.B.
for Gabriela and Tessa - D & F

First published in Great Britain in 1997 by Barefoot Books Ltd.
First published in the United States by Holiday House, Inc. in 1998

Graphic design by Denise & Fernando
Printed in Belgium

Library of Congress Cataloging-in-Publication Data
Blackstone, Stella.
Baby high, baby low / written by Stella Blackstone ; illustrated
by Denise & Fernando.
p. cm.
Summary: Depicts contrasting pairs of babies, including quick and
slow, happy and sad, and hot and cold.
ISBN 0-8234-1345-4 (reinforced)
[1. Babies—Fiction. 2. English language—Synonyms and antonyms—
Fiction. 3. Stories in rhyme.] I. Fraifield, Denise, ill.
II. Azevedo, Fernando, ill. III. Title.
PZ8.3.B5735Bab 1998 97-21371 CIP AC
[E]—dc21

Baby High, Baby Low

Written by Stella Blackstone
Illustrated by Denise & Fernando

Holiday House / New York

High, baby, high

Low, baby, low

Quick, baby, quick

Slow, baby, slow

Happy, baby, happy

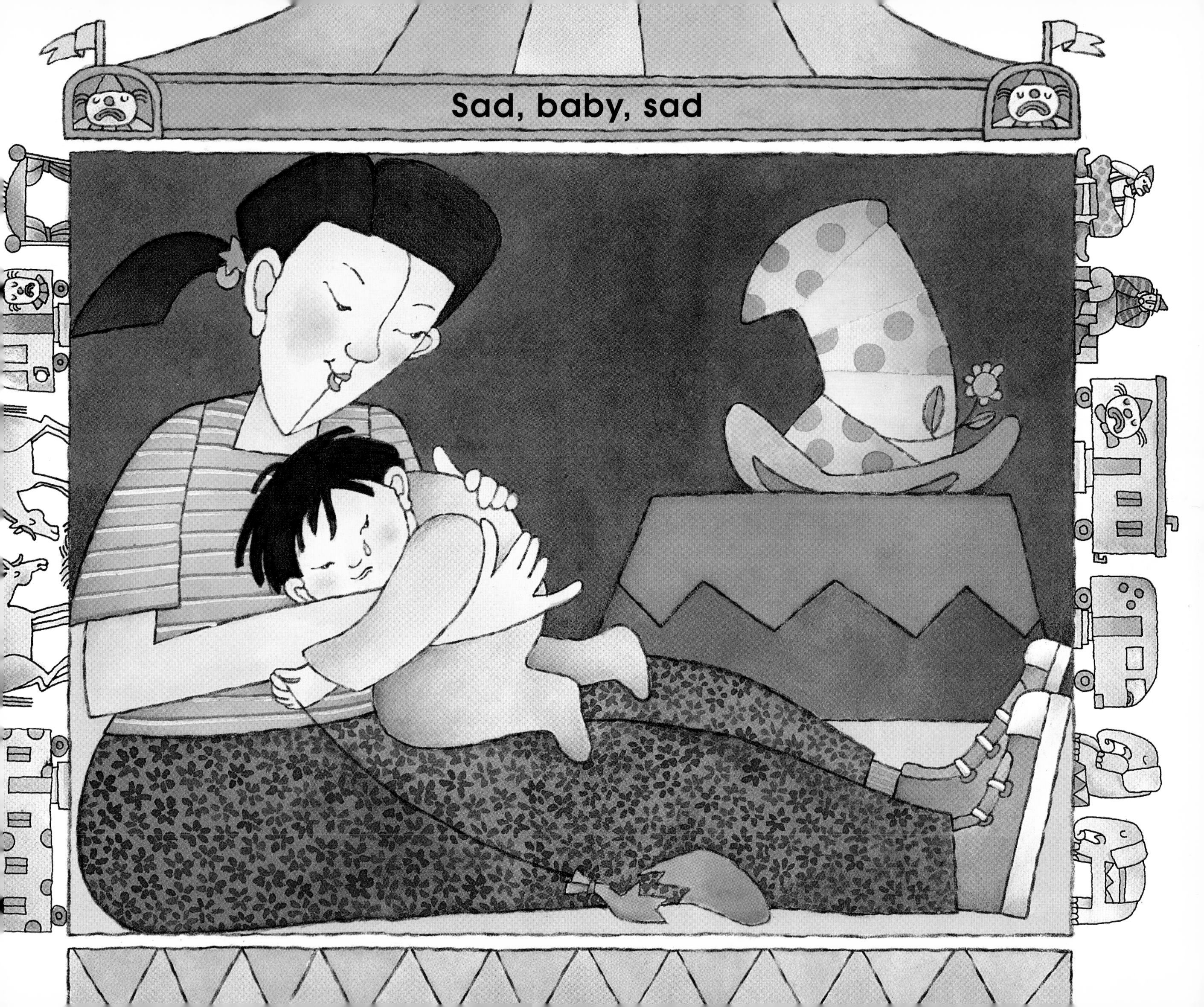
Sad, baby, sad

Good, baby, good

Bad, baby, bad

Hot, baby, hot

Cold, baby, cold

Shy, baby, shy

Bold, baby, bold

Big, baby, big

Small, baby, small

Short, baby, short

Tall, baby, tall

Fat, baby, fat

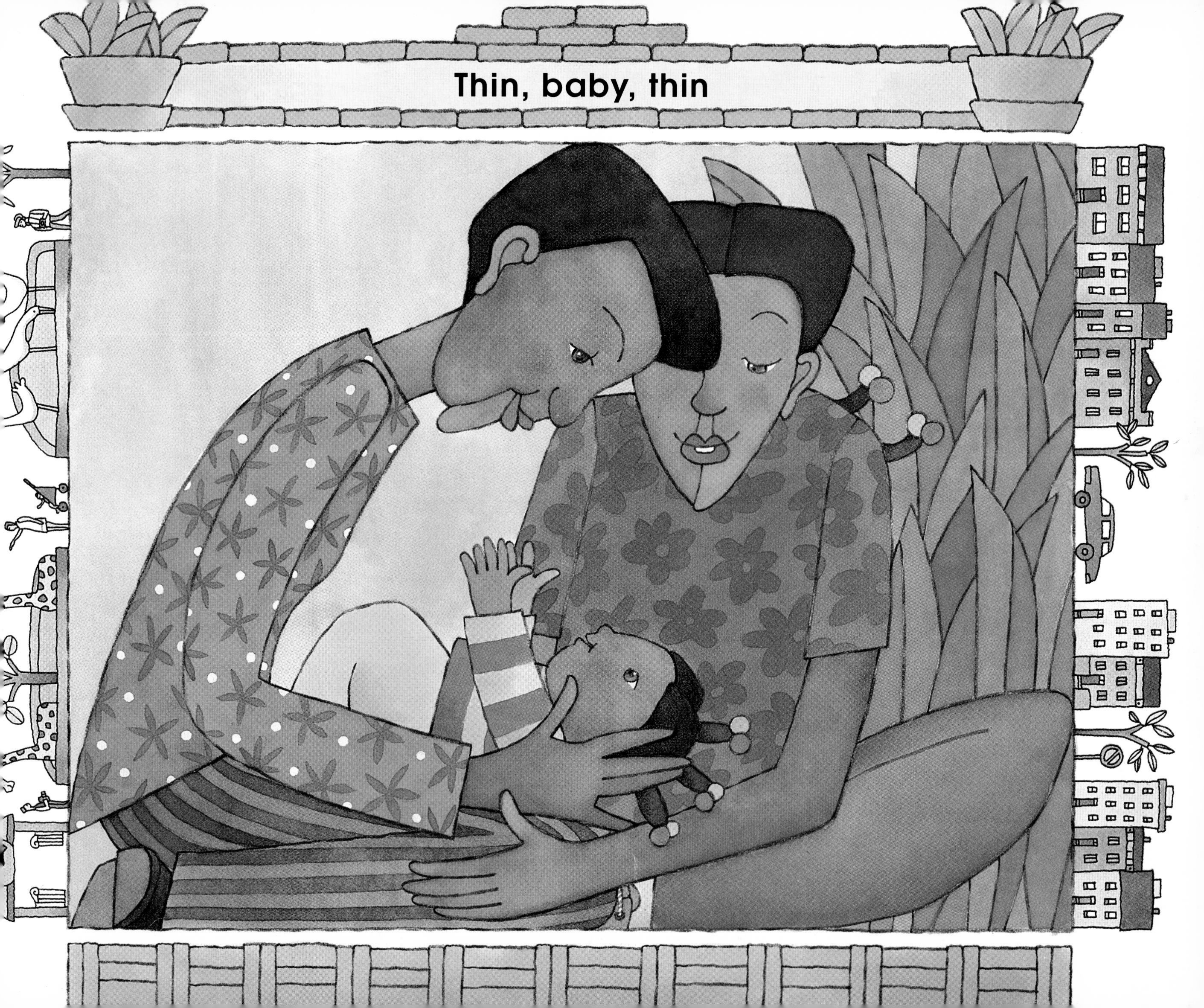
Thin, baby, thin

Out, baby, out

In, baby, in

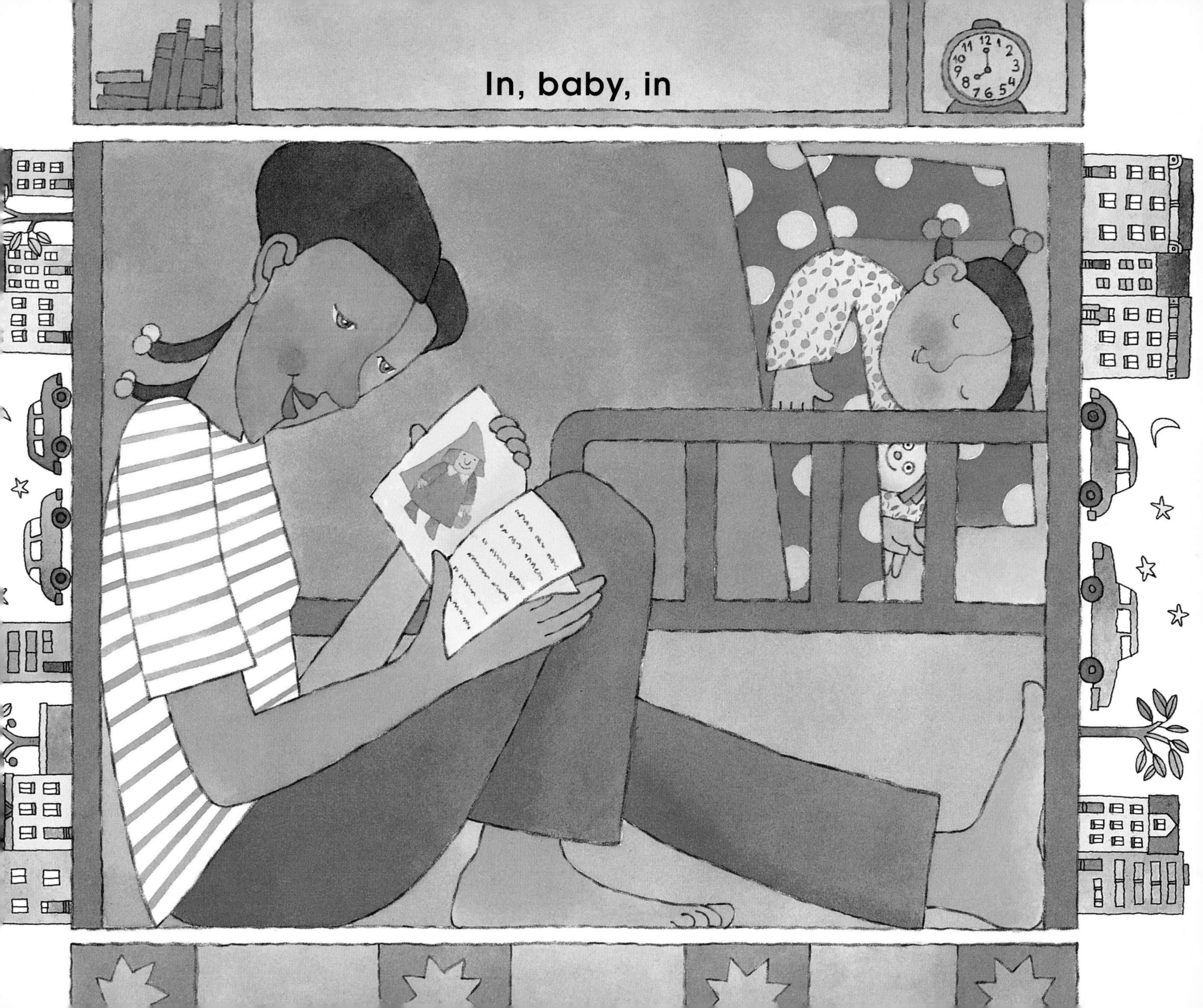

Stella Blackstone is the author of *My Granny went to Market: A Round-the-World Counting Rhyme*, illustrated by Bernard Lodge and *Baby Rock, Baby Roll*, which is also illustrated by Denise and Fernando. She is a freelance writer who lives with her three children in England.

Denise Fraifeld and **Fernando Azevedo** are natives of Rio de Janeiro, Brazil, who studied at Pratt Institute and now live in Brooklyn, New York, with their daughter Gabriela. They illustrated Stella Blackstone's *Baby Rock, Baby Roll*.

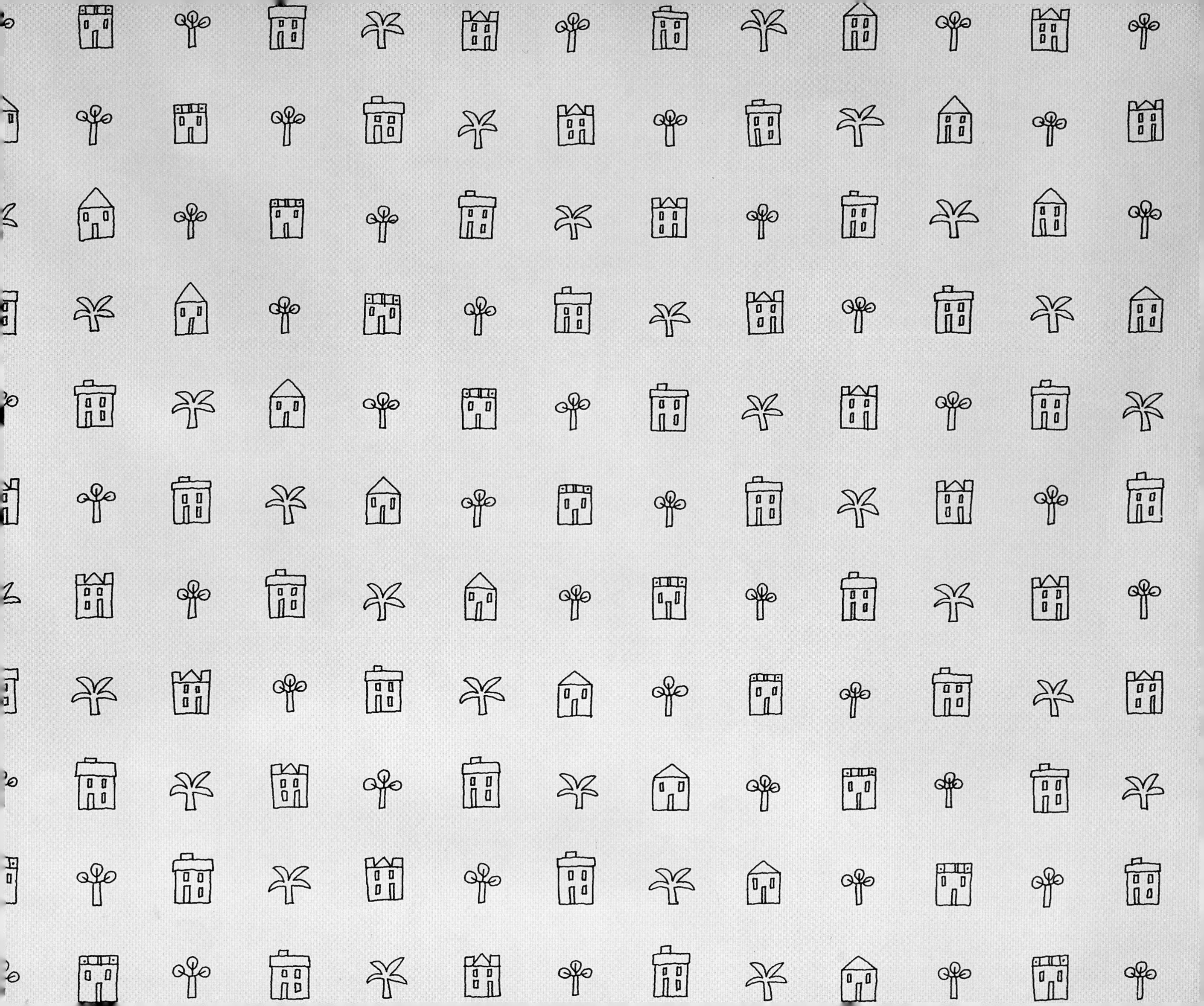

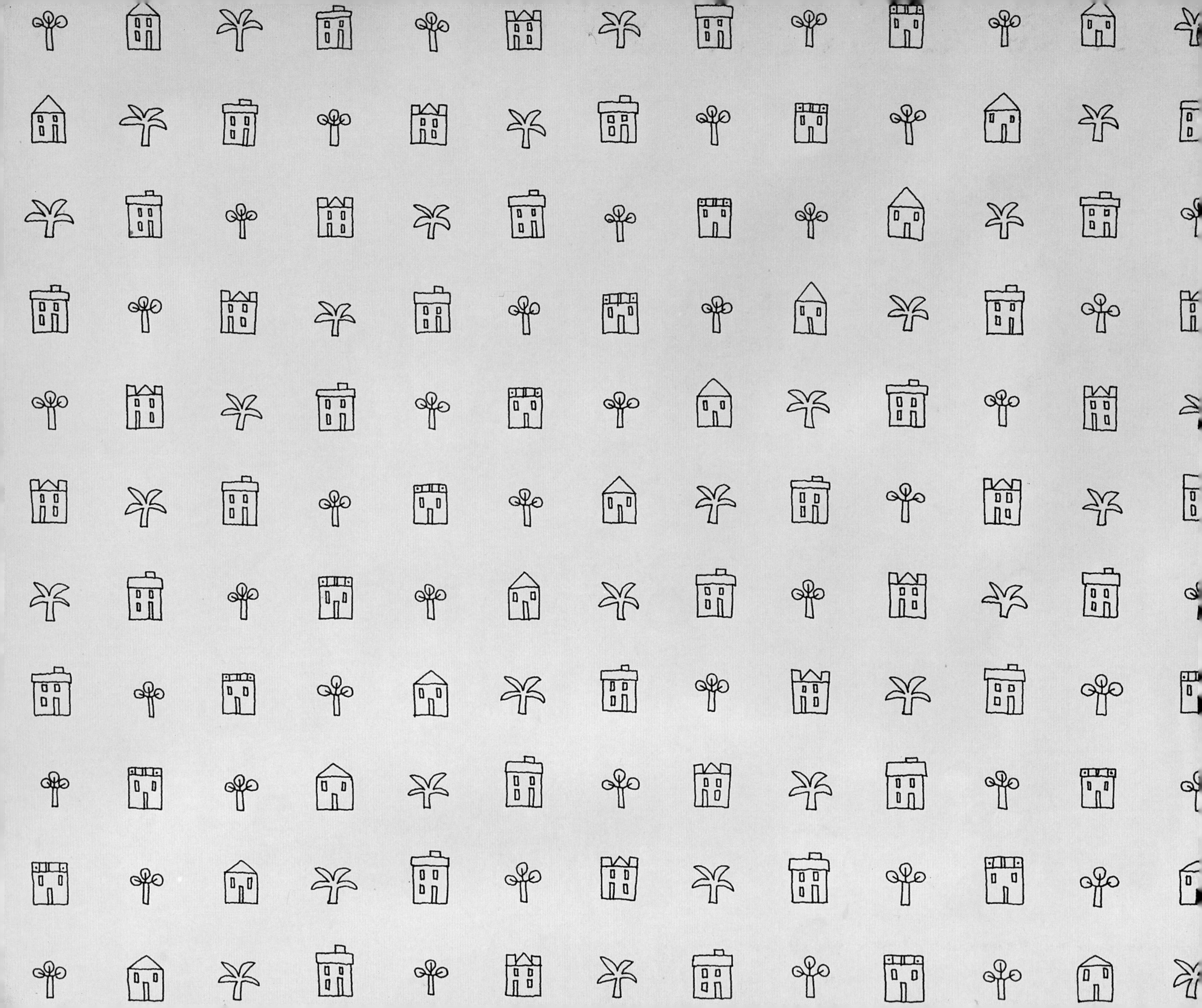